George Sibscota

The deaf and dumb man's discourse

A treatise

George Sibscota

The deaf and dumb man's discourse
A treatise

ISBN/EAN: 9783337257958

Printed in Europe, USA, Canada, Australia, Japan

Cover: Foto ©Andreas Hilbeck / pixelio.de

More available books at **www.hansebooks.com**

THE
DEAF and DUMB MAN'S
DISCOURSE.
OR

A Treatise concerning those
that are Born DEAF and DUMB,
containing a Discovery of their
KNOWLEDGE of UNDER-
STANDING; as also the Method
they use, to manifest the sentiments of
their Mind.

Together with

An Additional Tract of the
REASON and *SPEECH*
of *Inanimate* Creatures.

By *GEO. SIBSCOTA.*

LONDON,
Printed by *H. Bruges,* for *William Crook* at
the *green Dragon* without *Temple-Bar.*
1670.

A DISCOVRSE

Concerning thofe that are born

DEAF and DUMB,

And of their

K N O W L E D G E.

1. **S**Uch is the calamity of Mortals in this ftate of mifery, that they are invaded on all fides not only when they are born, by a vaft army of Difeafes, but are alfo troubled with many diftempers whilft the Womb is their Lodging; there we often meet with the precurfory meffengers of Death even in the very beginning of Life ; and whilft the formative faculty is framing this machin of our immortal Souls, fome deformity, fome irregularity in the ftructure, or other preternatural difpofition

B   pofition

position obstructing the exercise of the parts immediately intermixeth it self with our birth.   Which enormity of the parts, or constitution repugnant to the Lawes of Nature, prejudicing the operations, and contracted at our Birth, some have been so scrupulous as to think that it ought not to be called by the name of a Disease, but of a Defect, reserving the name of Disease for the defects of that which was once perfect.

2. And as this kind of defect is found to be in many members of man's body; so it most frequently happens to the sense of Hearing :   Which was *Aristotle*'s Observation long ago, who therefore in the first of his Problems, Sect. 11. moves this very question ; Why the Hearing, of all Senses should be most prejudiced from our Nativity ?   And submits it to Consideration, whether this may not be the reason or cause of it, because the Hearing and Voice seem to be derived from the same principle :   For

Speech

Speech (faith he) which is a kind of Voice, may eafily be depraved, and not without great difficulty reftor'd to its perfection; a fign whereof is, that we continue mute for fome time after we are born (for in our Infancy we cannot fpeak at all) then at length we begin to ftammer; fince therefore Speech may be eafily perverted, and that the principle of Hearing and Speaking is the fame (for, faith he, 'tis the Voice that is the *primordium* of Hearing) it follows confequently, that, that Hearing, of all the Senfes is fooneft corrupted, as it were *per accidens*, not *per fe*. We may (faith he) lay this down as an Argument taken even from other Creatures, that the principle of Speech may be eafily deftroyed; for no other Creature can fpeak; but Man folely is endued with this faculty; yet he (as is premention'd) is a long while, before he begins to fpeak.

   3. We will propofe to our felves
thrce

three things to be throughly weigh'd
in reference to this confideration of *A-
riftotle.*Firft,the reafon it felf,by which
he maintains,that the Senfe ofHearing
may be eafily injured from the very
Birth above all the reft of the Senfes;
becaufe, the principle of Speaking or
of articulate fpeech may be eafily
prejudiced , the principle of Hearing
being the fame ; and therefore Hearing may be injured from the Birth
not *per fe,* but as it were *per accidens.
viz.* by reafon the common principle
of Speech and Hearing may be hurt.
Secondly, we will take into our Confideration, that which follows by confequence from that very reafon ; to
wit, that the Hearing is never dam-
nified from the Birth, unleffe Speaking, or the articulate enunciation of
the Voice be fo likewife : becaufe
there is a certain common principle
belonging to the Speech,as well as
Hearing, which being injured , it
neceffarily follows that both of them
muft be prejudiced.   This confequence

quence was fo certain in the opinion of *Ariftotle*, that in his fourth Book of the History of *Animals*, *chap.* 9. he ingenioufly pronounceth, That they who are born Deaf, are alfo Dumb; and for that reafon they may make ufe of a Voice, but not of Speech. Thirdly, we will fubjoyn and inquire into their Underftanding that are born Deaf, as alfo the way and manner of their Knowledge. Fourthly and laftly, we will Contemplate a litttle upon the reafon, and difcourfe of brute Animals.

SECT.

SECTION I.

*Why is Hearing, of all Senfes
foonest prejudiced.*

4. **A**S to the firft, *Ariftotle* layes
down a certain common prin-
ciple of Hearing and Speech : But
doth not fufficiently declare what, or
what kind of thing that is : Indeed
he affirms that Voice is the principle
of Hearing, as well as of Speaking,
and withal faith, that the Hearing
and Speaking feem to proceed from
one and the fame Principle. And
truely the Voice is the material principle of Speech, as far as the articulate fpeech is framed by the Voice;
as if the fame Voice were the principle by which the Hearing is ftirred
up

up to the act, or the Hearing had an actual being by means of the Voice, as *Peter Apponenfis* explains the meaning of *Ariftotle.*

5. But this principle will not effect our Defign, for this queftion will remain unfolv'd, why, where there is a Voice in Deaf men, yet there is no Hearing? and where thofe that are mute can frame a Voice? or brute Animals themfelves, yet they cannot fpeak by virtue of that common Principle? And wherefore fince Infants can hear, fhould they not alfo be able to fpeak by the affiftance of that common Principle? For the particular caufe, either of the obftruction of Hearing, or impediment or depravation of Speaking, is on either hand to be fought in the organs: the irregularity whereof, the vitiated conformation, or folution of the continuum, or the convenient influx of the animal fpirits being impeded by any defect of the organ: obftructs the operation thereof. But we will fee in our fol-

lowing Diſcourſe, whether there may not probably be ſome other principle found out, that depends upon the mutual conjunction of the nerves.

6. But the reaſon why New-born Babes can hear, but not preſently ſpeak, or pronounce articulate words, is, becauſe there is more required to the framing of ſpeech, or ſpeaking, than to the reception of a ſound, or hearing. For, the Hearing is meerly paſſive, and the Sound arriving at the organ of Hearing (which is the very auditory Nerve, expanded to the internal parts of the windings of the *Auditorium*, preſuppoſſing a convenient diſpoſition of the outward, as well as inward parts of the Ear) a Sound is immediately repreſented : but 'tis not the ſame when a Voice is uttered, the Speech is not immediately framed, or Diſcourſe raiſed, nor doth it meerly conſiſt in paſſion.

7. Brute Animals that have Lungs and the *Aſpera Arteria*, are able to utter a Voice, otherwiſe than thoſe
other

other Creatures, that onely make a Sound or noife; but yet they cannot therefore fpeak.

The *Dolphin*, faith *Ariftotle*, in the 4th. Book of *the Hiftory of Animals c. 9.* hath Lung and the Arterie, and therefore can utter fomewhat of a Voice, but yet hath not a free and voluble Tongue, nor Lips by which it might frame any articulate voice; therefore it only makes a noife and muttering.

8. But thofe that have Lips and a greater liberty of the Tongue, fo as to be able to frame fome one articulate Word (as Sheep do the word βῦ, Oxen and Cows μῦ, *&c.*) yet they cannot frame their Voice to feveral articulate words; for all Brutes want that aptitude of the organs, by which articulate words are made and formed; though there are fome brute Animals that do imitate the words and voice of Man : Of which hereafter.

9. But Infants and Children, though they

they have that aptitude of organs naturally, by which an articulate Voice may be pronounced, yet the use of those organs is not then made so familiar to them, as truely to frame words : for there must be exercise, and from thence a habit contracted to speak easily and readily ; just as when a man in time hath gained a habit, he sweetly playes upon a musical Instrument

10. Besides, the organs of Infants are then but infirm, and by degrees arrive to perfection. when Nature, or the innate heat by little and little consumes the superfluous moisture. And so *Aristotle* in his last forequoted place is in the right, where he saith, that as Children cannot rule and govern their Limbs, so their first impotency and imperfection appears in the Tongue, and 'tis long before they are freed from it ; which is the reason that for the most part they stammer, and speak with difficulty. And hence it is that Infants cannot properly be said

to

to be mute, becaufe there is no priva-
tion, but in a fubject that is capable
of the habit, yet they may properly
be faid to be born Dumb, whofe organs are fo difpos'd from their Nati-
vity, as that they have an ineptitude
to fpeech when grown in years.

11. But this property of the organs, as the Tongue, Palate, Lips,
Teeth and Throat, is only beftowed
on Man to the end that he may get a
habit of fpeaking any thing. Though
herein alfo is great variety by reafon
of the Countreys and Kingdoms, in-
fomuch that all men have not a ready
pronunciation of all Letters in ufe
with other Nations : Thus the guttural Letters are appropriated to the
Eaftern people ; and among them a-
nother, though no guttural letter called *Dad* (which is pronounced like
ddfh) is fo peculiar to the *Arabians*,
that they can diftinguifh any forein
Nation from their own, by the pronunciation thereof ; though they con-
verfe with them never fo long, and
the

the *Arabians* are meant by thofe that pronounce this Letter exactly, as when they fay that *Mahumed* was the moft Eloquent of all that pronounce the letter *Dad*, that is, of the *Arabians*. The fame is every where obvious in the *European* Tongues : for, it is a matter of difficulty for the *French* to pronounce the *German G*, which is pronounced like the pointed *Kef* of the *Perfians* or *Turks* ; hence it is that they cannot without difficulty pronounce the *German* monofyllable *Tang* : and fo in the reft.

12. As to the reafon or caufe why the Hearing of all the Senfes is fooneft prejudic'd from the Birth, that cannot by any means be referred to any common principle of Hearing and Speaking ; becaufe fuch a principle cannot be judged a fufficient principle of Hearing only, or it conferrs no o-therwayes to the hearing then *objetti-ve*; in regard that at leaft it cannot poffibly fall under the notion of the efficient caufe, by which there is any

per-

perception of the Voice ; therefore there muft be fome other reafon or caufe found out of the thing in queftion, if we hold it fimply true, that the Hearing is fooneft injured from the Nativity.

13. But the genuine reafon of the thing muft be found in the winding and truely labyrinthean ftructure of the inward part of the Ear, which may be foon perverted or obftructed; into which the *more* tender Nerve hath a *mæandrous* paffage, which alfo is foon affected with the fmalleft thing and from the filth of thofe humors which defcend thither partly and primarily proceeding from the moifture of the Brain.

14. Befides the drum of the Ear may it felf be more groffe from the Birth, than ordinary, or be overfpread with the finews of the Brain, or fome other groffe humour ; or there may be fome thick membrane that may cover the auditory *mæanders* ; but they, to whom this happens, are onely troubled

bled with thicknefs of hearing, and do as it were receive the found by the Mouth, the reafon whereof fhall be given in our following Difcourfe. And fometimes there may be fome peculiar defect in the ftructure of the Ear, extending it felf to the Jaws and Palat of the Mouth, which is the reafon that thofe that are Deaf ufe to fpeak thorough the nofe, as *Ariftotle* affirms in his fecond and fourth *Problem f.* 11.

SECT.

SECT. II.

*Whether thofe that are Born Deaf,
are Dumb alfo?*

NOw we come to the examination of the fecond point, which feems to be the confequence of the former ; and which is confirmed by *Ariftotle*, in the 4. Book *de Hift. Animal. c. 9. viz.* That thofe that are born Deaf are alfo Dumb. And as this is diduced and laid down as a Propofition by *Ariftotle*, by reafon of the former Affertion , though againft reafon : fo it is admitted by very many, and thofe Phyficians too , as an univerfal truth, without any further fearch into the truth of the thing or difquifition of the difference. Hence they prefuppofing posing on all hands, as a thing beyond exception, That all those that are born Deaf are likewise Dumb. (as *Sanctor. comm.* in *Art. Medic.* and *Galen Part 2. Question* 41. are also of opinion) make an inquisition after the cause only of the thing supposed, or incontrovertibly true : But we will more narrowly difcuffe the *Thefis* before we pry into the cause, why it often falls out to be so.

16. Indeed, if by those that are Mute we underftand such whofe organs have in themfelves an ineptitude to the framing of an articulate Voice, it is an abfolute miftake to maintain that all that are born Deaf, are Dumb alfo : for the ineptitude of organs to the framing of Speech doth not immediately follow the want of Hearing. For where deafnefs depends not fo much upon the defect which is common to the Hearing and Speaking, (which we have allowed may fometimes happen) as upon the imperfection rather peculiar to the very *adæquate*

quate organ of Hearing (of which as there are many parts, so there may be many obstructions, that may destroy the Hearing) it doth not follow therefore that there is an immediate inability to speak.

But why rather as the Hearing is sometimes destroyed after the birth, the speech remaining perfect, so also at the very birth, or immediately after, may not such a constitution of the Organs happen, whereby they may be adapted to the forming of speech, and yet be incapable of Hearing?

17. Here we must consult with experience, which testifies that those that are born deaf, may learn to speak. For so *Vallef. Philofo. Sacr. cap.* 3 reports, that one *Peter Pontius* a Monk of the Order of St. *Benedict,* and his Friend, taught those that were born deaf to speak, by no other way, than instructing them first to write, pointing at those things with his finger that were signified by those Characters, and then putting them forward to

C

that

that motion of the Tongue , that did correspond to the Charact-ers.

18. But if by those that are dumb we understand , such as have Or-gans fit for the forming of words, but yet understand no language , nor ever learn't such words as express the conceived sense of the mind ; it is undeniably true, that many that are born Deaf , are also Dumb, who never were instructed in any Tongue, or signicative words by the forementi-oned artifice, or some such kind of means.

19. Therefore as to the cause, why those that are born Deaf are also Dumb,(at least for the generality) *Albertus Magnus* in his 4. Book *de Anim.* Tra&. 2. C. 2. saith, that those that are Deaf from their Nati-vity are also Dumb,because they could learn no Idiom by the sense of Hearing. And *Sanctor* in Art *Medic*. approves of this opinion. *Galen part*. the 2. *Questi-on* 4. as also *Bartholinus* in the 3.

book

book of his *Anatomy c. 9.* re-
ferring the cauſe of deafneſs to the
Drum of the Ear, who ſaith that thoſe
who from their birth are thus affected, are alſo for the moſt part Dumb,
becauſe they can neither conceive in
their mind, nor utter with their
Tongue thoſe words, which they never heard.

20. But *Laurentius* contradicts this
opinion in the 11th Book of his *Anatomy*
and the 11 th *Queſtion* where he ſaith,
I do not allow of that vulgar conceit,
that the reaſon why thoſe that are
Deaf are mute, becauſe they can learn
no language, and becauſe Hearing is
the Senſe of Learning; for then ſaith
he, if that be the only cauſe, why
Deaf Men are Dumb;

Firſt, Why do they breath out
their ſighs and groans, which are natu-
rall paſſions with ſo much difficulty?

Secondly, whether or no, might
not thoſe that are Deaf frame words
and ſpeches to expreſs the ſenſe and
conceptions of the mind, if they could

pronounce them, as well as thofe, who were the firft Inventors of them.

21. But in truth we may give this anfwer to *Laurentius* his firft argument, that it is a fallacy, to fay that Deaf Men groan and figh with difficulty; becaufe original deafnefs, hath no manner of communication with the parts fubfervient to refpiration. But *Laurentius* his miftake feems to be grounded upon what *Ariftotle* writes in his 4th *Problem. Section* 11. That deaf Men breath not without violence; by which *Ariftotle* doth not mean a violent or difficult refpiration which belongs to the Lungs and Breaft, but a vehement fpiration or breathing through the Noftrils; whereupon he addes, that the Noftrils become more large by the paffage of the Spirits, and thats the reafon they cannot fpeak but through the Nofe. And fo alfo in the fecond *Problem,* (faith he) Thofe that are deaf want but little of being dumb, and

and thofe that are dumb, fpeak through the Nofe, for their Spirits are driven that way, becaufe they cannot fpeak.

22. Now where there is a kind of ineptitude to fpeech in deaf Men, occafioned by fome defect appertaining to the Palate, as well as the Organ of Hearing, they breath not without difficulty; and becaufe their Spirits do bend their courfe more towards the Noftrils, by reafon of the widenefs of their paffage, befides that, they breath out a kind of voice with their mouths, as *Arifttole* fpeaks concerning Elephants in the 4. Book *de Hift. Anim. c. 9.* yet that found, they make with their Nofe, refembles the hoarfenefs of a Trumpet.

23. To *Laurentius* his fecond argument it may be replyed; although man by nature, though deaf, is arm'd with reafon to make him fit for invention; yet as *Plato* teacheth, it is not the property of a vulgar Genius to impofe names upon things, much lefs is it in the power of every perfon, to

invent an elegant fpeech or peculiar Tongue, to make the conceptions of the mind intelligible.

24. He that firft gave creatures their names, to wit, *Adam*, was in his integrity, and in the fupernatural ftate of innocency inftructed with fuch wifdome, as tranfcends the capacity of prevaricated nature : The confufion of various Tongues was afterwards fupernaturally fent by God at the building of the Tower of *Babel*; and then the variety of *Idioms* did gradually proceed from the commixture of Tongues, or had fome other rife by the common ufe and confent of men.

Yet thofe that are mute, can find out a way whereby to explain the fenfe of their mind to others, as well as if they had the faculty of fpeaking, which is analagous to fpeech, as fhall be manifefted in i'ts proper place.

25. But poffibly fome perfons beleive that if deaf men had in them that aptitude of Organs whereby they might be capeable of fpeaking, that they

they fhould ufe fome native Language,
or fpeech, which Nature their School-
Miftrefs fhould inftruct them : for fince
Sermocination is effential to man, as
fubordinate to reafon, fo it is not impro-
bable, that where the Organs are fo
adapted, there muft be granted external fpeech. To which we anfwer, that
'tis true the very faculty of fermocina-
tion, which is fubfervient to them in the
declaring the fenfe of their mind, by
thofe fignifications that are fet forth
by words, whatfoever they be, is effential to man ; yet the names of things,
and fo confequently the Languages
themfelves, or the *Idioms* of fpeech
are not to be learn't by nature, but
by inftruction, exercife and cuftome.

26. And really if any certain
fpeech did depend upon nature, as every individual perfon of mankind hath
one and the fame nature : fo all Nations whatfoever would ufe one and the
fame Tongue. But the contrary is
known experimentally. Therefore
their opinion is altogether vain and
foolifh,

foolish, who, being ignorant of *Phi-lofophy*, would needs oblige them-felves and others to this perfuasion, that if a Child were taught no Lan-guage in his Infancy, but left to his own conduct, he would fpeak *Hebrew*, that is, he would make ufe of this Language by the meer inftinct of Na-ture, which is a conceit altogether inept and foolish.

27. *Vallefius* in the forequoted place makes a good objection to this phan-taftical opinion; faying, If Speech were connatural to men, as many other things are; it would be fo, though they learnt any other Language, and con-fequently all men would underftand two Tongues. For, if the Speech in which a man was firft inftructed doth not hinder his learning another; (fince many men can fpeak two, three, or four Languages) much leffe can that which is natural, be impeded by that, which is acquifititious.

28. Nay rather, if one Tongue were natural to man, they could not be
docible

docible of all the reſt; becauſe that which is internal obſtructs the exter-nall.   Therefore as Nature made Man without Knowledge; that he might be capable of all Arts; it muſt neceſſarily follow, that ſhe Created him without any Language, that he might learn them all.   We alſo find that many men are more apt to learn other Languages, than the *Hebrew*; and that many *Europæans* attain the true pronunciation of ſome *Hebrew* words with no ſmall difficulty; which could not be, if the *Hebrew* were our natural Language; for all things do voluntarily tend to that which is natu-ral to them.

29. We conclude therefore, that they who are born abſolutely Deaf, though their organs are fit for the prolation of words, which frequently happens, yet they are for the major part, Dumb; that is, they cannot pro-nounce ſignificative words, becauſe they could not learn any *Idiom* by the Ear: For it is very rarely known
that

that they are taught to Speak by any such particular art as *Peter Pontius* made ufe of, which out of *Valleſius* we have before mentioned.

30. But in the mean time we do no way contradict, but agree with *Laurentius*, when he afcribes it to another caufe, why all thofe that are Deaf are generally Dumb, or at leaſt ſpeak with difficulty, taken from the mutual conjunction of the Nerves. For this we lay down, as another caufe why Deaf men born, are Dumb, and fo really dumb that they are altogether incapable of fpeaking articulate Words. For that communion of the Nerves confiſts not in this, that becaufe the Nerve of the fifth Conjugation which is the auditory Nerve, and the Nerves of the fixth Conjugation, which are thofe belonging to the Speech (or rather of the feventh, for this is the Nerve of the Tongue) are mutually pyned together within themfelves, before they are difperfed into their proper parts, as *Peter Apponenſis* in

in

in his Explanation of the *propos'd Problem*, is of opinion; or becaufe that the fame Nerves are originally invefted with the fame Tunicle , which in the judgement of others, is no.leffe repugnant to it felf; for the Nerves of either of the prementioned Conjugations are found by a fufficient and long interval originally diftant; and it cannot be faid, that they have any other common Tunicle, than what all other Nerves are covered with, *viz.* the *Pia Mennix* from which far-fetcht communion of the Nerves we may alfo inferr, that thofe that are Deaf, are Blind, and thofe that are Blind, Dumb.

31. But that Conjugation of the Nerves is well demonftrated by *Laurentius* (which is alfo mentioned by *Bauhinus* in the third Book of his *Anatomy c.* 22. 60. and others,) that the Nerve of the fifth Conjugation (commonly called the auditory Nerve) hath feveral branches iffuing from it, the larger whereof is expanded to the
Ear

Ear and the membrane of that moſt exquiſite ſenſe, and carries all ſorts of Sounds to the Brain, the leſſer extends to the Tongue and *Larynx*, and is there embraced by the ſeventh Conjugation.

32. And from this Communion of the veſſels proceeds the ſympathy between the Ear, the Tongue , and Larynx, and the very affection of thoſe parts, are eaſily communicated one with the other.   Hence it is, that the pulling of the Membrane of the Ear, cauſeth a dry Cough in the party ; which *Avicen* takes notice of : and that is the reaſon, moſt deaf Men, at at leaſt thoſe, whoſe deafneſs ariſeth from the ill-affection of the Nerves of the fifth pair , are Dumb, or elſe ſpeak with great difficulty ; that is , are not capable of framing true words, or of articulate pronunciation, by reaſon of the want of that convenient influx of the animal ſpirits ; and for this cauſe alſo , it is that thoſe that are thick of Hearing , have a kind of hoarce ſpeech.

33. In

33. In like manner, if there be any e-
vil defect which ufually confifts in the
inward ftructure of the Ear and the Palat (which makes them fpeak through
the Nofe, as we have before mentioned out of *Ariftotle*) there follows a
deafnefs and withall an impediment
of Speech, the organ of fpeech,
being vitiated, but not fimply, becaufe a Language cannot then be
learn't by hearing. But contrarily, if
the only ftructure of the Ear be de-
fective or only that branch of the fifth
pair, which is carried to the Ear be
preternaturally affected ; the Hearing
may be hindred, or Deafnefs may
arife ; but the impediment is but by
Accident ; becaufe that when Words
cannot be heard or received by the
Ear, they cannot be learnt.

34. But if the Hearing be prejudic'd by the defect of the *Tympanum*,
or by any particular Membrane that
is over it, that is a peculiar Accident ;
for in this cafe there happens to be a
thicknefs of Hearing, which is near-
eft

est of kin to Deafness, rather than an absolute Deafness it self.   And in such cases, those that are deafish use to hearken with their Mouth, or to suck in Words and Sounds with gaping, and so to pronounce without trouble those very words, by the help of those organs subservient to Speech, which they learnt by Hearing; and such are by no means to be call'd Dumb persons.

35. But the Sound flows to the inward part of the Ear, or the very organ of Hearing, by the help of the little *Cartilagineous* Pipe, which is conveyed from the second passage of the Ear to the Mouth and Palat, being appointed to convey the Excrements of the Ear through the Mouth, like an *Aquæduct.*

By the benefit of this Conduit-pipe it is, that we can exactly apprehend our own Words, when both our Ears are stopt; so also, if we hold a Stick in our Mouth, and therewith touch any musical Instrument, we hear the

sound

found thereof more exactly; and if you are desirous to know, whether there be any person approaching near you in the Night time, place one end of the Staff on the ground, and hold the other with your Teeth , you hear then far better, though at a great distance.

36. By the same Pipe, when we blow our Nose, or hold our Breath, by stopping of the Ears and shutting the Mouth, we are sensible that the air finds a passage into the Ear , by which the Membrane of the *tympanum* is struck with the outward sound, and sometimes prejudiced thereby , if it be very violent , and by this it is that Smoakers puffing up their Cheeks having taken in the fume of Tobacco, send it out at their Ears, so as that they seem to Breath at the Ears. Therefore the Opinion of *Alcmæon* is not ridiculous who held that she-Goats did Breath thorough their Ears, as *Ariftotle* hath it in his firft Book *de Hift. Animal.* *c.* **11.** And

to

to Physicians this conveyance doth insinuate , that masticatory Medicines are not to be slighted in the inward pains of the Ears.

S E C T. III.

Of their way of Understanding that are Born Deaf.

37. **B**Efore we come to the third point of what is to be dicufs'd concerning the propos'd *Problem* we muft Contemplate a little further on thofe that are Born Deaf, and fet with what Knowledge they are endued, fince men ufually gain the major part of what they know, by Hearing.

38. Firft, thofe perfons that are Born Deaf, and have the Vifive faculty intire, they may gain the Knowledge of all Vifible things, as vifible and may frame thofe univerfal con

D   ception

ceptions of them by the abftraction of the Mind, as well in this cafe, as where the Hearing is perfect : Nay farther, and thefe perfons as well as all other men in general may proceed from things Vifible by the light of the Underftanding to the Knowledge of the Invifible myfteries of the Deity ; fo that they are left inexcufable, as well as any other perfons whatfoever, if they do not glorify God, and return him thanks for Benefits receiv'd : Of thefe the Apoftle fpeaks *Rom.* I. *v.* 20, 21.

39. Furthermore, if thofe that are Born Deaf, are alfo Blind, although they are depriv'd of the knowledge of many things, which come within the compafs of the Senfes, nor can arive at the knowledge of God by the outward Book of Nature, as the other, yet they may obtain the knowledge both of God and themfelves, by thofe notions that are grafted in their minds. And it is very probable, that thofe whofe Intellects are

are less disturbed in Contemplation by the appearance of corporeal things; the implanted Seeds that are in them of the Knowledge of Divine and immaterial Beings, do easily break forth into action; as we our selves are more apt for the search and Contemplation of Divine things, the less we are distracted by outward objects, and the fancies that result from them.

40. Certainly it is not at all consentaneous to reason, that the rational Soul, or Mind is altogether unactive in such persons, and lies as it were lurking in the lethargy of a benumm'd security, or that they do not according to their capacity incline their minds to the Knowledge of the Deity, by virtue of that innate light that is in them, as well as the Celestial Angels, and Divels; since the Soul is to be reckoned in the number of Intelligences (though perhaps placed in the lowest rank of Intelligences) and in reality is not so deeply plunged in matter or matterial fun-

ctions

&ctions, by reafon of its defect of Sight and Hearing.

41. But what is to be thought of thofe who are born Deaf, as to their Knowledge in things that concern the Myftery of our Salvation ?

Thefe things as they are too fublime, either for Univerfal , Humane , or Angelical knowledge, cannot be found out, or underftood by thofe notions implanted in the mind. And as *Faith comes by Hearing,* according to the A-poftle, where this is wanting, it may poffibly feem very agreeable to truth , that there can be no Faith, and there-fore no faving knowledge ; and the confequence is undeniable, fince no man can be faved without Faith.

42. Oh this is indeed a very hard faying , which fhipwracks the Soul ! Truly fince thofe that are born Deaf are no more guilty of neglecting the means of their Salvation , than In-fants (concerning whom however the Sacred Pages advife us to be more charitable) what reafon I wonder can

there

there be, why we should think God less merciful to them, who are also born of faithful Parents, than to Infants! We will leave the disquisition of their Faith, or the manner thereof to Divines. Hath God therefore, who according to his Will hath elected some one of all Mankind corrupted by the Fall, to be Vessels of mercy, and others Vessels of his wrath, strictly registred all those that are born deaf in the number of those that are Vessels of wrath? Yet God's Promise and Covenant belongs to these, as much as to the children of the faithful.

43. The Holy Ghost in truth is the chiefest cause of Faith, who begets it in our hearts by the preaching of the Word, and consequently by Hearing. This is the ordinary way of God which he commands us to follow; he that neglects this, is excluded from Faith by his own fault. Yet God is not wholly tied up to this one way of operation. He hath extraordinary ways which we are ignorant of, and

he

he will not reveal to us.   Yet God
made ufe of peculiar means to bring
St. *Paul* to the chriftian Faith, and
made him of a Perfecutor of the
Church, become an Apoftle, *Acts.* the
9. He proceeded after another manner to the converfion (at leaft in part)
of the Eunuch of *Candace* the Æthio-
pian Queen. Acts the 9. viz. *By the
reading of the word of God.*

44. And fhall we judge that no
perfons can be faved, that live where
there is no publike preaching of Gods
Word, and fo by confequence where
the mind gains no fpiritual knowledge
by Hearing ? May we not affirm, that
by diligent reading, and co-operation
of the Holy Ghoft, Faith may be en-
gendred in the Souls of the Godly ?
Now therefore if this means be without Hearing, why may not God manifeft other ways, that fo at leaft his o-
peration may not be confin'd to the
hearing folely ?

45. But let us examine whether
there are not other means appointed by
God,

God, by which thofe that are originally deaf, may attain the knowledge of
divine Myfteries fufficient for falvation.

There is no neceffity, why fpeech,
which is ufually acquir'd by Hearing,
fhould precede writing; but fpeech
ufeth to be in the firft place by reafon
of it's facility, for thofe that have all
their fenfes perfect, are more apt to
fpeak, than write. But where there
is a defect of Hearing, they may begin with writing, and fo by writing
come to fpeaking, as is manifrft by the
fore-cited example out of *Vallefius*.
Now external fpeech is a kind Meffen-
ger or rather reprefentation of the internal, or of the intellect it felf.

They therefore that are born Deaf
may by writing inform their minds
with the knowledge of thofe things,
which muft be obtained by hearing in
others, whofe fenfes are all perfect ;
and fo they may make ufe of writing in
lein of fpeaking, which is otherwayes
attained by Learning ; and they as
Vallefius fpeaks in his third chapter d*e*

*Phil.Satr.*Do gain the knowledge of Divine things by the fight, which others do by hearing, which I my felf (faith he) can teftify, in thofe Scholars which my friend *Peter Pontius* undertook, who firft taught them that were born Deaf to write, or to exprefs the conceptions of their mind by writing, and then to fpeak.

46. The fame reafon there is for thofe that are born Deaf, if Dumb alfo; they may by writing underftand things, although no external writing is fubfequent to fpeech; for the fpeech in Man conduceth not to the gaining of knowledge to themfelves, but only to communicate the Conceptions of their own mind to others. This is clear by an example taken out of *Fel. Platerus* who in the firft book of his Obfervations *pag.* 118. reports, that a certain perfon who was born Deaf and Dumb, could with Chalk draw out his mind in a Table-book, which he carried continually about him, and underftand what others writ therein.

47. But

47. But as writing, or the reading thereof, may serve in stead of speech, by which the Conceptions of the mind are laid open to the sight, as well as they are by speech to the Ear ; so there may be other signs made imitating the outward speech, and Succedaneous to hearing ; as those are which Mutes themselves always make use one in lieu of speech, and by which they conceive the Sentiments of other mens minds. For experience teacheth us, and there are also many obvious examples among us, that those that are originally Dumb, and Deaf do by certain gestures, and various motions of the body as readily and clearly declare their mind, to those with whom they have been often conversant, as if they could speak, and likewise by such gestures of other Persons, they do absolutely understand the intentions of their mind also.

48. The Emperour of the Turk maintains many such Mutes in his Court ; who do express the
Con-

Conceptions of their minds one to another, and as it were interchange mutual difcourfe, by gefticulations, and variety of external fignifications, no otherways than we that have the faculty of fignifying our own thoughts, and conceiving thofe of other Perfons by outward Speech. Nay the Turkifh Emperour himfelf, and his Courtiers, take great delight with this kind of Speech fhadowed out by geftures, and ufe to employ themfelves very much in the exercife hereof, to make them perfect in it.

49. *Cornelius Haga* Embaffadour to the Emperour of the Turks fent thither by the States of the United Provinces did once invite all thofe Mutes to a Banquet (as I obferved from the relation given me by the moft Noble and Worthy Dr. *Brinkins* Senator of *Hardervick*) where though there was not a fyllable heard yet they did exchange feveral difcourfes, as is ufual at other Treats, which the Embaffadour underftood by an Interpreter on both fides

by

by whofe affiftance he himfelf did difcourfe with the Mutes upon all fub-
jects.

50. But thofe very fignifications of
things, which Mutes make ufe of,
proceed not from nature, but from
their own inftitution no more, than our
fpeech; Therefore they attain unto
them by Study and exercife.

Although however moft of them do
fhadow out fome outward manner, of
the things which they aim at. As
when they clofe one hand, and move
it up towards the Noftrils, thereby
they fignifie a Flower. Now the fignifications of thofe Mutes (which is as it
were their Speech) are not like the
Languages which vary among feveral
Nations, nor are fo abfolutely different.

51.And as the Mutes do by their geftures exactly and diftinctly underftand one another, and thofe Perfons
alfo that ufe fuch a kind of analogous
Speech among them; fo they conceive
many things by the geftures, motion
of the Lips, and fuch like things in
thofe

those that really do speak, and sometimes understand a great part of their
conceptions by such outward things.
So saith *Platerus* in the place above-
mentioned: that his Father told him,
that that Deaf and Dumb man (whom
we discourst of a little before) when
he very devoutly heard *Oecolampadius*
Preaching, did apprehend many
things from the motion of his Lips,
and gestures; and so from others.

52. And there is now at this very
time in the City of *Gronning*, such a
one who being born Deaf and Dumb,
constantly frequents publike Sermons,
and doth as it were contemplate upon
the Words of the Preacher with his
eyes fixt upon him, so that he seems
to receive them in at his Mouth as o-
thers do by the Ear. This person
when he earnestly desires to receive
the Holy Sacrament, I do not at all
question, but that he hath that knowledge of those Divine things, that concern his Salvation, insomuch that he
cannot be debarr'd from it without
                              some

fome fcruple of Confcience. Although I am of opinion that he ought to be examined as to this his knowledge and Confeffion, which may be done, by means of his Wife, or Servant, his Interpreters, whom he alwayes hath with him, and who difcourfe with him very nimbly by figns, of any thing whatfoever.

53. We will fubjoyn one example out of *Phil. Camerarius,* which is in *Horæ Subcifivæ* 1 *Cent.* 37. 'We have now among us (faith he) a young Youth and a Maid born of the fame Parents, and indeed of a Noble and honeft Family, who have an extraordinary acutenefs of Wit: and though Nature brought them forth Deaf and Dumb, yet they can both of them Read diftinctly, Write an excellent hand, and keep Merchants Accompts. And as he dextroufly perceives by a Nod what you would have him to do, and ifhe wants a Pen, will exprefs himfelf by geftures; and is very cunning at all Games

'that

that are usually plaid among us upon the Dice, which cannot be man-
aged without great subtilty; so she
very much exceeds all Maids at her
Needle and curious Weaving. But
among other their admirable qualifications, which Nature hath be-
stowed upon them; this is wonder-
ful, that they seem to understand
what any one speaks by the motion of
the Lips; Wherefore they are often at Church, hearing the Word
Preacht. So that it will be no ab-
surdity to say, that 'tis probable
they take the Words in at their Eyes,
they are so intent, which others use to
do by the Ear. For they can at plea-
sure without any suggestion, or o-
ther help write the Lords Prayer,
and other pious Oraisons. And can
remember the Gospells appointed
to be read on Holy-days as well as
others, and readily Write them.
And if the Holy Name of *Iesus* be
mentioned in the Church, he, a-
bove all the rest, will in a posture

‘ of

of Reverence uncover his head, and
bow the knee. "Thus Nature like
an indulgent Mother was folicitous
and ftudious to recompenfe their defects, that fhe might free her felf
from the injurious accufation of a
cruel Step-mother.

The Fourth SECTION,

Being

A DISCOURSE

Concerning the

REASON,

AND

SPEECH

O F

BEASTS.

54. THe/e things, concerning tho/e that are born Deaf and Dumb being thus determined , we will proceed

ceed to a further Illuftration of the
reft which occurr in the *Problem* propos'd, and the Explication thereof
And the third point which *Ariftotle*
hath offered, to our meditation con-
cerns the *Speech* of *Beafts*, where he
lays down this, as an Affertion.

That the faculty of Speech (which
prefuppofeth reafon) is only beftowed up-
on Man, and that no other Creature can
Speak : Which we will take into our
Confideration.

55. To fpeak truly, the inward
Speech is no more, than the *nuncius* or
a certain image of internal reafon,
which goes to the *Idea* of the reafon
expreft; whence the *Græcians*, and that
not without reafon, call *rationem* and
fermonem, Reafon and Speech by the
fame name λόγον abfolutely, *i. e.*
Speech which the Philofophers diftinguifh into ἐνδιάθετον & πεοφοεικὸν into internal and external, and the one muft
neceffarily accompany the other, unleffe there be an imperfection, or defect in the organs. Therefore this is

E

a neceſſary Conſequence, That where there is no Reaſon, there can be no external Speech; and ſo on the contrary.

56. And 'tis from this ſtrict copulation of *Reaſon* and *Speech*, that Τὸ λογικὸν *rational* is expreſs'd in the *Arabick* Verſion, by the word *Natthack*, which ſignifies Speaking, *Gen.* 2. *v.* 7. as its oppoſite Ἄλογον, irrational, *Chares*, which ſignifies Mute, is ſo named in 2 *Pet.* 2. *v.* 2. to which the *Dutch* phraſe anſwers, *een ſtom Beeſt*, (and our *Engliſh* exactly, *a Dumb Beaſt*) *i.e.* an irrational Creature.

Nay, the Holy Scripture calls irrational; *dumb Creatures*, or *Creatures without Speech*, 2 *Pet.* 2. *v.* 16. where the *Aſs* of the Prophet *Balaam* is ſaid to be Ὑποζύγιον ἄφωτον ἀνθρώπου φωνῇ φθεγξάμενον, *ſubjugale mutum humana voce locutum*; which our *Engliſh* Tranſlation renders, *The dumb Aſs ſpeaking with Man's Voice*.

57. But here our *Galen* ſuggeſts a difficulty, who, whilſt he ſeems to deny

ny

ny Brutes external Speech, yet he affirms, that they have Reaſon, from
whence external ſpeech indiſputably
proceeds ; ſo that if any Brutes have
fit organs for the uttering of articulate words, it ſeems that they muſt
not be denied external ſpeech, reaſon or ratiocination being ſuppos'd ;
For thus *Galen* expreſſeth himſelf in
the beginning of his Book intituled
Exhort. ad Art. lib. Stud. It is not
yet certain, whether Beaſts, which
are called Brutes, are altogether void
of Reaſon. For though peradven-
ture they have not that Reaſon in
common, with us, which is underſtood
by the Voice, and call'd denunciative
yet certainly, they all of them have
that which is taken according to the
Soul, which they call Reaſon, capable of Affections in common, as well
as we, though ſome more, ſome
leſſe.

§. But here we muſt make a halt
for a while, to the end that we may
more exactly determine what is to b

thought

thought of the Reason of brute Beasts commonly so called, and also of their Speech.   Indeed the most profound 'Philosophers, *Porphyrius*, *Plutarch*, ' and *Galen* (saith *Bodin* in *Theatr.* '*Nat. lib. p.* 476.) have proved ' by almost an infinite number of Ar- ' guments, that Nature hath bestow- ' ed Reason upon Beasts.   And *Huartus in Scrutin. Ingen. ca. 6.* 'There 'is no doubt (saith he) but that brute ' Animals have a Memory and Phan- ' tasy, and a certain Power besides, ' which is correspondent to the In- ' tellect, as an Ape resembles a ' Man.

59. How many things do we meet with, concerning the Ingenuity and Reason of Brutes (of which *Plutarch* hath writ a peculiar Treatise, as also many things are mentioned in *Gryllo*) as well by Tradition from Authors, as those which are obviously known to us, which certainly seem to argue some kind of Reason, or somwhat analogous to Human Reason.

Pro-

Prodigious things are related of the *Elephant* by *Pliny*, *Ælian*, *Plutarch* and others, which *Lipsius* hath Collected out of several Authors in his *first Century ch.* 50. Where among many other observable things this following Story, which is almost beyond belief, yet faithfully quoted out of *Acosta*, and *Garcias ab Horto Hist. Arom. lib.* 1. *c.* 14. relates it also.

There was an Elephant in the City of *Cochin*, who wanting his food at the precise accustomed hour, complained, and bray'd. His Master excused it by shewing him that the Brazen Vessel, which usually contained his food was leaky and run out, and that the occasion of this delay was, because, that it could no longer hold his Drench or Wash : And therefore commands him, if he would eat, to carry it to the *Braziers* to be mended. He obeys, takes it upon his Trunk and brings it to the *Brazier*. Who either through negligence, or to make fport with the Beaft, did not mend it well, and ftop up the Chinks.   The Elephant brings it back again, his Mafter fpying the fault, grew angry, and exclaimed both againft him and the Elephant; and in fine, bids him carry the Veffel back again.   He doth fo, and with a querulous tone throws it at the *Brazier.* He being a pleafant fellow, endeavours to put a Cheat upon him the fecond time, and makes, as if he did ftop the holes, but did not :   Yet he mift his aim; for the Elephant was fo cunning, as to carry the Cauldron to the River, and there puts it into the Water and fills it, to try whether it would hold, but he found that it did run out.   He being hereupon highly incenfed, runs back to the *Brazier,* and bellowed out with a thundering voice, fo that the Neighbours came about them, and among the reft the King's *Vice-roy.*   The *Brazier* pacifies the Beaft with fair words (and here faith *Lipfius,* I know not whether

ther I dare proceed any further) and at laſt he takes the Veſſel into his hands and mends it well and ſtrongly. But the Elephant being miſtruſtful, carries it again to the River and fills it with Water; when he ſaw that it would hold, he turns himſelf to the ſtanders by and ſhews it, calling them as witneſſes to the matter of fact; and ſo went home.

61. *Garcias* adds further, who travelled into thoſe parts, that there are ſome yet living, who affirm they ſaw it done. And he teſtifies, that Elephants do not only underſtand the Language of their own, but alſo thoſe of forein Countreys, if taught them. And a little after; In ſumme, there is nothing wanting in this Creature to make him appear rational, but only Speech : although this alſo (as the ſame *Garcias* witneſſeth) is by ſome attributed to it. Of which hereafter.

62. And leſt that any one ſhould make a doubt of what is reported concerning Elephants; hear *Iac. Bontius*

an Author of very great credit; who was some few years past in the *East-Indies*, and chief Physician to the *Belgian* Society, and himself an Eye-witnesse thereof; who, in his Notes upon the forementioned place in *Garcias*, declares expresssly, That whatsoever is said of the Elephants docility; is true : The same things in some measure are related by *Pliny, Scaliger, Camerarius, Lipsius* and others, concerning the tractablnesse and ingenuity of *Dogs* and *Horses*, and also of their fidelity to their Masters, which almost exceed all belief; and yet are every where made manifest by daily experience.

63. There was in *Holland* not many years ago, a comely *Horse* carried about by a fellow to be seen; being by custom brought to that which *Scaliger* mentions of another in his 209 *Exercitation*; who did very strange things, at his masters command, or single Nod; among other things being commanded to shew him the greatest

wencher

wencher, or drunkard, &c. in the Company, he was not much out of the way, being without doubt, directed by some private sign from his Master.

64. *Scaliger* in his 236 *Exercitation*, reports, That he saw a Dancing *Parret*, who did with the gesture of his head, and by hanging down and fluttering of his wings imitate a *Savoyard* (that was a Songster) dancing; which he assures us a *Crane* did also very pleasantly.

Ionstonius in Thaumat. Natur. reports of another *Parret*, that she would say over the Apostles Creed before the Cardinal, and answer questions. Also of another that belonged to *Henry* the Eighth King of *England*, who being fallen into the River cried out for help, and promised twenty pounds to those that would save her, but being taken up, he bid them give the man a Groat.

65. I my self at present, have a little *Dog* at home, who not long ago seeing the *Cat* licking a large Ladle

dle that was hung up by the Chimney;
he first leapt at her, and endeavour-
ed to drive her away by barking; but
she fell still to her work not minding
him, by accident he finds me out a
great way off from that place, runs to
me, and ever and anon fawns upon
me with his forefeet, and then runs
towards the *Cat*, as it were to shew
me his meaning, that I might see her,
and drive her away; so that the
Whelp took notice of this unworthy
act of the *Cat*, though not used to do
it, and would out of envy have her
driven away. I had formerly another small Cur at *Hardervick*, who
would very hardly be kept at home
when I went abroad, insomuch that
if he had slept in the Kitchin at any
time longer than ordinary, being un-
certain, whether I were gone out in the
interim, or no; starting up of a sud-
den, he would run into the Parlour,
and look about for my Cloak, which
as soon as he spied, he returned into
the Kitchin satisfied, gathering as it
were from hence, that I was in my Study, and so as yet within.   66.

66. We may daily obferve, the geftures of *Apes*, and their imitation of Mens actions without any fraud or deceit, though not accuftomed to it formerly. *Oornithographer* affirm that *Cranes* obferve a kind of difcidline in their flight, and keep a Watch or ftand Sentinel. Every dayes experience openly proclaims the admirable ingenuity and policy of *Bees* and *Ants*. The Spinning of *Spiders*, and the way they have to enfnare *Flies*, or trap them fometimes unawares. I omit a thoufand other obfervations of brute Beafts, that are daily obvious to our fenfes, which do feem to declare that there is fome *Idea* of Reafon, or fome kind of ratiocination in them.

67. I will only annex one thing which *Fort. Licet. lib. 2. de Monft. c.* 68. relates out of the *Portugal* Annalls of *Caftanenda*; to wit, That a certain Woman for fome Crime was by Sea tranfported to a Defart Ifland, when fhe was fet a fhore there, a horrid company of *Apes* (which that place

place abounded with) came and
ftood round about her; and that there
was one among them bigger, than the
reft, to whom all gave place; who
taking the Woman very gently by
the hand led her into a vaft Cave,
and that he and the reft, did fet before her ftore of Apples, Nuts, and
variety of Roots, and with a comple-
mental Nod invited her to Eat; at
length fhe was Ravifh'd by the Beaft,
who continued the act a long time, in-
fomuch that fhe had two Children by
him; and that fhe lived in this miferable condition for fome years; till
(God commiferating her cafe) a *Por-*
tugal Veffel was driven thither, and
the Soldiers coming a fhore for Water, which they had out of a Foun-
tain next adjoyning to that Cave, and
by great chance the *Ape* being abfent,
the woman ran to the men, having feen
none of that Sex a long time, and falling
fuppliantly at their feet, befeeched
them to free her from that wicked and
miferable fervitude; they pittying her
con-

condition, did condefcend to her intreaties, and fhe came aboard of them. But behold, faith he, the *Ape* unexpectedly coming after her, and with ftrange geftures and noifes calling back his Confort, and yet no Confort   VVhen he faw them hoife up the Sailes, he runs back with great fpeed, and brings one of the Children and fhews it to the Mother, threatning to throw it into the Sea, unleffe fhe would return ; and did fo immediatly ; then he runs back to the Cave, and returning to the Sea-fhore with the fame fpeed fhews the other, threatens, and then drowns it; and at laft he himfelf fwims after her, and was drowned.

68. As to the Speech of Brute Animals; 'tis confirmed by daily experience, that fome of them may by cuftom imitate in fome meafure an articulate Voice, or Humane Speech. This is a very familiar obfervation in the *Parret, Pie,* and *Sterling. Plutarch, Pliny, Ovid,* and others, teftifie

fy the ſame thing of the *Nightingal*. I my ſelf (ſaith the Author) have obſerved (at *Merſa* in my native Countrey *Anno* 1646. at the Houſe of the moſt Noble and Strenuous Gentleman *wilhelmus Reinerus a Clou*, who was a Peer and Governour of that City and County) in that kind of Finches, which they call a *Goldfinch*, and *Ariſtotle* χρυσομέλης, that could imitate Man's Speech articulately and diſtinctly enough : This little Bird was ſo accuſtomed by heartng people ſpeak frequently, that as often as ſhe did prepare to ſing, ſhe would utter theſe words diſtinctly, *Sing Manneken*, *ſing man*, but in a lower tone, as it ſhe were hoarſe; and after ſhe had often repeated them, then ſhe would proceed with a moſt ſweet harmony.

We have given you an account of the *parret* that could rehearſe the Apoſtolick Creed; and of the other, that falling into the River deſired help and promiſed a reward, in the fore-

going

going part of our Difcourfe.

69. We will not here take any notice of the *Serpent*'s difcourfe with *Eve*,
immediately after the Creation, *Gen.*
3. nor of the Speaking of *Balaam's*
Afs, *Numb.* 22. and 2 *Pet.* 2. *v.* 16.
becaufe we are fatisfied that the one,
was done by Diabolical, and the other,
by Divine operation; we will only
briefly infift upon thofe things which
the Naturalifts, as *Pliny*, *Ælian*, *Plu-*
arch, and others, report concerning
the Speech of *Elephants*, and of their
writing too. Among which poffibly we
might reckon the ingeminated Words
that were heard to be fpoken by the
Statu of *Iuno Moneta*, and *Fortuna*,
as *Valerius Maximus* reports, but that
the more inward receffes of Nature
are firft exactly to be difcuffed by
us, that we may the more clearly dif-
cern the illufions of Satan from the
Works of Nature.

70. Concerning the peculiar
Speech of *Elephants*, *Oppian* deliver-
eth himfelf, as followeth;

φήμ,

φήμη δ'ὡς 'Ελεφαῖτες ἐπ' ἀλλήλοις λαλίωσι,

φθογγℓιὼ ἐκ σομάτων μερσπῖιδ'α τουπρίζοντες.

'Tis fam'd, that Elephants *with their own*
  kind
Talk, and in proper terms express their
  mind.

Acosta affirms (who lived a long
time in *East-India,* and did diligently
examine the nature and towardness of
Elephants, and receiv'd it from those
who made daily observations of their
nature) That in the Kingdom of *Malabar,* 'tis a general received opinion,
that these Creatures do Talk one with
another.

71. Nay, it is believed that they can
learn Humane speech, and express
their inward conceptions by familiar
Words. There was (saith the same
Acosta) an *Elephant* in the City of
Cochin, who did, at his daily work in
the Haven about marine affairs; who
though tir'd, was however urged by
                              the

the *Præfect* of that City, to draw a light Veſſel, (or Pinnace) into the Sea, which he had already begun to do, but the Beaſt refuſed it, and he preſt him with many fair words; and at laſt (not prevailing) he intreated him to do it for the King of *Portugal's* ſake. At which (O incredible!) the *Elephant* being mov'd (ſaith *Acoſta*) repeated theſe two Words *Hoö Hoö*; which ſignifies in the Tongue of the People of *Malabar*, *I will, I will*; and drew the Ship into the Sea without any further delay.

72. *Garcias ab Horto* in the place above mentioned, ſaith, That there are ſome People in *Cochin*, who affirm they ſaw a publike Regiſter (called *an Atteſtation*) which did mention, That there was an *Elephant* there that could Speak, and did ask his Governour for food, but he anſwered, that the Cauldron in which he boyl'd Rice for him was full of holes, *&c.* which ſtory is related before by *Lipſius* out of *Acoſta*.

73. But let us speak something of the Writing of *Elephants*, which is a representation of the external speech; *Pliny* out of *Mucianus*, reports, that one of these Creatures learnt the *Greek* Letters, and Writ in that Language, *Ipse ego hæc scripsi & spolia Celtica dicavi.*

And *Philoſtratus*, They write (saith he) and Dance, nay, to the Pipe also. But *Ælian* saith, I my self have seen an *Elephant* Writing the *Roman* Letters in a Table-book with his Trunk, and that withal, they were writ very even, not crooked; Nay, whilſt he was Writing, his Eyes were earneſtly fixed upon the Table-book, that you might plainly say, they were intent and accuſtomed to Writing.

74. Although the major part of Brutes have no articulate Voice, and so do not make use of Speech properly so called : Yet we see on all sides, that they expreſs their inward conceptions one with another, and with Men also, by the Geſtures,
Sounds,

Sounds, and Noifes which they make with their Bodies, and fuch other kind of means; even as Dumb Men ufe gefticulations and various motions, in lieu of Speech, whereby they dif-courfe very fignificantly among them-felves, as well as with other perfons.

75. Hither is to be referred that of *Philoftratus* in the Life of *Apollonius,* in his 4. Book *ch.* 1. concerning the *Sparrow,* who, as a meflenger, by the raifing of his chirping tone, did fig-nify to the reft, that he had found out fome place, where there was good ftore of fcattered Corn, and fo did com-municate the food he had difcovered to the reft of the *Sparrows,* who hear-ing that Voice of his, they all ma-king a fudden noife, immediately flew after him.

The like example was related to me by the moft Noble and renowned *Brinkins, p. m.* Burgomafter of *Har-dervick* when living, concerning a *Goofe,* who when fhe had found in any of the Fields a Stock of Corn, took her flight immediately to the rest of her Conforts, and making a noise among them, the whole Flock followed her, she flying foremost, and shewing the rest where their food was. We may daily obferve in *Dogs* greater remarques whereby they fignify their inward fenfe to others.

76. And fince it is fo, what muft we think of the Reafon of Brutes, and their *Sermocination* whatfoever it be? What is there wanting to make them rational Creatures, or make them accounted to be of Humane fociety? Are we not bound to acknowledge that there is in Brutes a kind of analogical Reafon or eftimative faculty that refembles Reafon, from whence their Ingenuity is derived, and by virtue whereof, they feem to be in fome refpects prudent.

77. And truely fince we fee that Brute Animals do fometimes Rave, and Dote (for *Apes* when Drunk, have a kind of *delirium*; *Dogs* are troubled with the *Hydrophobia* or Madnefs,

Madnefs, which happens (as is reported) to *Horfes,* *Oxen,* *Affes,* and
Camels) it muft needs alfo follow ,
that they have Wit, and the ufe of
Reafon in fome meafure ; for natural Potency and Impotency are to be
referred to the fame fubject : Hence
we find, that as that analogical Reafon is in fome, more exquifite and vi-
gorous , fo fome Brutes differ from
others in Ingenuity. Prudence, Docility and Stupidity. Of which Sub-
ject I have varioufly Difcourfed in
*Theatr. Natur. Univerf. part. 2. Dif-
putat. 5. f. 29.* and the following
Sections.

78. Yet this Reafon of Brutes is
abfolutely different from Humane
Reafon in its very effence, for the former is a kind of fenfitive or material
faculty of the Soul, to which , that
which is vulgarly called Cogitative in
man, or the eftimative faculty it felf,
illuftrated with Reafon , from the
prefiding , and hypoftatical union of
the rational Soul with the fenfitive,
F 3 Body

Body, doth in some measure agree : and yet this very Cogitative faculty in Man, though it be material, it is far more noble and excellent, than the Reason in any species of Brutes can be; and doth by many degrees surpais the Reason of *Elephants*; then this Reason is apprehended to transcend the Reason of *Gallus Africanus*, insomuch that there is herein a kind of irradiation, or a represented Image in Man, flowing from the Immortal Soul, which also by its Native and Essential Reason is capacitated to imitate the Coelestial Intelligencies ; which bright light of Reason in Man communicates it self to the estimative faculty ; by reason of the intimate connexion of the Rational Soul with the Sensitive Body, by which the whole *Suppositum* becomes Rational.

79. And therefore 'tis not without reason that *Aristotle* saith in the First Book of his *Ethicks* to *Nicomachus*, the last Chapter; That Man hath a two-

twofold Reafon; the one, he hath principally in himfelf, *viz.* τὸν νῦν the very Mind or rational Soul : the other, that he is obedient to Parents, and that he hath Reafon by participation, to wit, that which he calls in Man τὸ ἄλογον or that part that is without the Humane Soul, as the Senfitive faculty ; this firft Reafon of Man is the very Intellect it felf, fo call'd by *Ariftotle*, which he faith, 3. *De Anim. cap.* 5. *t.* 20. is feparable, immortal, and impaffible ; the latter, the paffive Intellect, which he doth not affirm to be immortal and eternal, becaufe it perifheth with the univerfal fenfitive faculty, when the rational Soul is feparated from the Body.

80. The former fort of Reafon in Man, which is proper to the rational Soul or Mind, and is its native faculty, as the Mind of Man is an immaterial fubftance, not at all enveloped in matter, fo that makes ufe of no corporeal organ in the exercife of its functions ; but foaring above all the

Senfes,

Senses, contemplates upon Divine, Immortal, and Eternal Beings; and understands those things which no Sense of the Body can conceive; and still desires that which the sensitive faculty wholly abhorrs. So that *Calvin* in the first Book of his *Institutes c. 5. S. 5.* reprehends those (and that not undeservedly) who being addicted to preposterous subtilties would fain wrest that saying (which teacheth that the Faculties of the Soul are organical) to a contrary sense (*viz.* from the sensitive faculty, to the very rational Soul) as well (saith he) to destroy the immortality of the Soul, as to rob God of his proper right : for (saith he) because the faculties of the Soul are organical : by this pretext they so link it to the Body, that it cannot subsist without it.

81. The latter Reason of Man, which is communicated to the sensitive or estimative faculty by participation, as it is not corporeal, nor intermixed

termixed with the Body (as *Ariftotle*
fhews *de Anim. l. 3. c. 4. text 6.*)
becaufe that it is a kind of communicated image, and reprefented as it
were in the Mirror of the Mind; fo neither doth it ufe any organ in its operations (according to *Arift.* in thefore-
cited place) although 'tis bufied about
outward appearances, as the object of
its operations, and can underftand nothing without them (as *Ariftotle*
teacheth *c. 8. text 39.* And in truth
that which he hath in the laft quoted
place, belongs to this paffive Intellect, or rather to Man, as he is of a
fenfitive nature, adorned with an a-
ctive Intellect; that an Intelligent perfon muft Contemplate upon outward
Phænomena, according to that common
faying, *Nihil eft in Intellectu, quod non
fuerat prius in fenfu.* Nothing can be
in the Intellect, that hath not been
firft received by the Senfes.

82. For this fenfitive faculty in
Man, though illuftrated with Reafon,
underftands nothing of it felf, but is
like

like a blank Paper, or Book, that is ſuſceptible of any inſcription, 3. *lib. de Anim.* 4. *text* 14. for it is capable of all things that are cognoſcible, by virtue of that light which darted from the rational Soul, whereby it is illuſtrated, and extends it ſelf to all material, immaterial, individual, abſtracted, Mortal and Eternal objects.

For as it is ſenſitive, it perceives *v. g.* the Water, Fire, Fleſh, Magnitude and the like; and forms an imagination of them (which is alſo common to Brutes, as well as Men) but ſince Fleſh is one thing, and the Eſſence of Fleſh another; Magnitude, is one thing, and the Eſſence of Magnitude, another; and ſo of the reſt; it doth by another part of it ſelf, or by it ſelf in another capacity (*viz.* not as it is ſenſitive, but cogitative, or as it partakes of Reaſon, and is enlightned by the rational Soul) diſtinguiſh the Eſſence, from the things themſelves, which fall under our Senſes.

8 3.

83. But the former Reason of Man, or the genuine faculty of the rational Soul, as it is altogether immaterial, so it challengeth a Knowledge proper and natural to it self, not any way proceeding from Matter, or the Senses of the Body (For there is not alwayes one and the same, but a different reason of the supernatural Knowledge of Divine Mysteries, or of those things which exceed our Human Capacity, and want the support of Faith) whilst in the *interim* it renders that very Knowledge which is drawn from the Senses and inferiour Reason far more illustrious, and more clearly discerns the truth it self.

84. For this genuine faculty of the rational Soul, hath within it self the connate principles and seeds of all manner of Knowledge (which do not involve Divine Mysteries) or else is furnished with such an Understanding, that it can extract the truth of things out of their Womb by discourse and ratiocination. So also the know-

knowledge of God is engraven in the minds of men, yet not. so, as if every man did acknowledge a Deity, or that the existence of God is as it were written in their minds so soon as Born (of which opinion *Anselm* and *Hieronymus* were, according to *Suarez Disputation* 19. *S.* 2. ◊. 3.) but that by Nature there are such principles of a Deity implanted in our minds, and such an intellectual light connate with them, that we may by the strength of our own Genius, without any assistance from the Senses attain the knowledge of the Power and Divinity of the Supreme Deity. Just as we do truly assert, that Geometrical truths are connate in us, though we do not originally understand the *Elements* of *Euclid*.

85. And as the dull and rude Vulgar, who use not to abstract the Mind from the Body (and therefore have no other knowledge but what is exerted by the Senses, and the dictates of inferiour or cogitative Reason) under-

understand and conceive the invisible things of God from the Creation of the World by Works, so that the τὸ γνωστὸν τῦ Θεῦ that which may be known of God (as our Version hath it) in the *first* to the *Romans* may be understood by the very *Plebeians* ; so Philosophers and such as are conver· sant with more sublime Speculations, or have learnt to free their minds from this terrene incarceration, attain unto the knowledge of the Deity by the inward qualifications of their minds, without being obliged to the testimony of Sense.

And really those very seeds that are naturally planted in the minds of men, do sometimes so powerfully exert themselves into action, that they bind the very Consciences of the most obstinate, and such as deny the very dictates of Senses. And herein we may affirm with *Calvin*, in the first Book of his *Institutes*, *c.* 3. ⸹. 1. That beyond all Controversy there is by a natural instinct, a kind of sense of the
Divinity

Divinity in the mind of Man, for God hoth endued all perfons with the Intelligence of his Deity, that no man fhould fhelter himfelf under the pretext of Ignorance, who by a conftant recollection of his memory, furnifheth him with frefh inftillations.

87. But as to the Reafon of Brute Animals ; being it depends upon the fenfitive Soul, it is abfolutely material, and drowned in the Body, it is altogether infeparable from it, and perifheth with the *Individuum*, and therefore is converfant with nothing but what is Corporeal and Mortal. The fame faculty is in all the fpecies of Brutes imployed about fome certain and determinate object, to which all of them are hurried by a natural propenfity ; and not as it is in Man, indifferent to any thing. So Nature inftructs *Swallows* to build their Nefts of Clay ; Beafts to get Coverts or Dens ; *Dogs* hunt the *Hare* ; and *Cats* watch for *Mice* ; which neither the Reafon of a *Cow*, nor an *Afs* prompts them

them to; nor can they by Art be brought to it.

88. And although probably some species of these Brute Animals are more freely exercised, about various objects by raciocination, than others, as we find in *Elephants*, *Apes*, *Monkies*, the *Cynocephali*, and *Dogs* themselves, and the like; yet they are apprehensive of the objects themselves no otherwise, than under the notion of singulars: For they perceive the Water, Fire, Flesh, Magnitude and the like; and then frame some fantasms of these very things; and these they, either compound or divide, and so judge or esteem of the species so receiv'd : but Flesh being one thing, and the Essence thereof, another ; Magnitude, one thing, and the Essence thereof, another, &c. as *Aristotle* speaks, they cannot discern the Essence of things from the things themselves, nor can they abstract individuals from universals. So that their universal Reason consists in particular and material things; and there.

therefore they are incapable of Learning, which is comprehended under certain Maxims and Rules.

89. Befides if it could poffibly be maintain'd, that fome Brute Animals have a kind of Senfe of Divinity (it is reported that that Idolatrous Religion confifting in the Worfhip of the *Sun, Moon,* and *Stars,* did proceed from *Elephants*) or that fome faint image or fhadow of Piety may be diftill'd into them, yet by that they cannot conceive any thing of God, unleffe it be by corporeal reafon, and fo have no Conception of God, nor can they ever be able to difpute concerning God by the deduction of Caufes, or by the fucceffive end, nor by conclufions drawn from the principles imprinted in their minds; but only by the fingular commodity or ufe, or the more fplendid appearance of the particular individual body, *viz.* of the *Sun* or *Moon,* and fo they cannot apprehend the invifible things of God, but can only frame a conception

tion or imagination of the corporeal *Idea* of thofe things which proximately move the Senfes.

90. Undoubtedly that which is purely Incorporeal and Divine, or which is the true Eflence of Divinity, which is only Religioufly to be Worfhipped, cannot fall under the apprehenfion of a faculty meerly corporeal. But if there do appear in *Elephants*, as well the fhadow of many Virtues, as a certain kind of imaginary *Idea* of Religion (as *Lipfius* hath heaped together many Examples out of divers Authors to that purpofe) what wonder is it, that the Celeftial Bodies ftrike the Senfes with greateft admiration and yet are not exquifitely apprehended by the Senfes, that that reprefentation of Religion whatfoever it be, fhould be directly apprehended? And fo they be believed by *Plutarch* and *Ælian*, to Worfhip the *Rifing Sun*; and by *Pliny* and *Ælian*, the *New Moon*.

91. Finally, the Wifdom of Brutes

confifts only in that part wherein they alfo fuffer a *delirium* ; but Man's Wifdom alfo confifts in the mind or active Intellect, in which they never dote, and herein they evidently differ from Beafts, who have not this faculty. So that that paffage of *Hippocrates, Aphor. 6. Sect. 2.* belongs only to the paffive Intellect, fo far as it refides in the fenfitive faculty ; where he faith, That thofe who are troubled in any part of the Body, and are hardly fenfible of the pain, their mind' (*ἢ γνώμη* or as *Galen* interprets it in his Commentary *ἡ διάνοια*) is' diftempered, for they are deceived by a defect of the inward Senfes , which Brutes have in common with Men, and ftand alwayes in need of their Miniftry, whilft tied to the fetters of the Body.

92. Therefore Men are truely faid to be diftinguifhed from Beafts by Reafon ; becaufe Brute Animals have not any foot-fteps of that Reafon that is natural to the rational Soul ; or the active

active Intellect ; but they only have some kind of shadow of that Reason which is communicated to the sensitive faculty, or of the passive Intellect ; so that they are said to have Reason Analogically.

93. Now as to the Speech which is apprehended to be in some Brutes, that have organs fit for the emission of an articulate Voice ; what kind of Reason that may be, and how it difers from Humane Speech; is the hing to be discussed ; And as the peech of *Parrets, Crows,* and other Birds, wo are taught by Art, is nothing else, but a certain articulate Voice without any mental understanding, to which they are trained up by Custome, not knowing for the most part what is signified by this or that word. So that *Parret* that rehearsed the Apostles Creed ; did not at all understand the things signified by those words. And therefore this sort of speech, is not at all a representation of the intrinsick reason, and so conse-

quently

quently no true fpeech.

94. But if fometimes it fo fall out that they feem appofitely to appropriate the Names of things to the things themfelves, or retain the fignification of them, that is the work of the Memory, by which they do accommodate thofe things which they by their docility have gained to particular things, as they have been accuftomed to them, and according to their often repeated appellations : But their fpeech extends no farther to other things, than Cuftome hath directed them. And as that *Parret* which fell into the River call'd for help, and promis'd a Reward, it muft neceffarily be, that fhe had by practice learnt thofe words being oftentimes before in the like danger.

95. And fince it is undeniable that not only *Elephants*, but fome other Creatures, as *Dogs* and *Horfes* (though thefe are not altogether fo capable) do in fome manner conceive the Speech of Man, to which they are accuftomed

ed, or underſtand what is meant by ſuch and ſuch words, as they are taught (and as they by the motion or geſture of their Maſters, know what they would have) though ſome more exactly, than others. Is it a greater wonder for theſe Brutes, if they have organs fit for Speech, to be able by outward expreſſions (as they have learnt by Cuſtom) to ſignify the ſingle conceptions of their eſtimative faculty to others, which they frame within themſelves according to the common ſpeech they are accuſtomed to, than that they ſhould by the uſual geſtures of the Body, and other various ways (which is alſo the Speech of Mutes) be able to adumbrate their inward conceptions to others ? Or what wonder is it for a *Parret*, *Pie*, *Crow*, or *Starling*, to expreſs what they inwardly conceive or deſire by an articulate Voice, or ſuch as they have learnt by cuſtom ?

96. And thoſe Creatures that have been us'd to Speech can count number?

bers ; and yet they have no formal
conception of those numbers ; because
that cannot be done but by abstract-
ing, and so consequently by the immaterial faculty.　For in the num-
bring of any thing proposed , or the
collecting a definite multitude out of
unities, it is requisitely necessary that
the mind have an *Idea* of some numbers , and so that the abstracted number be known, and that it appear, how
the third differs from the fourth, and
the fourth from the tenth , and so on ;
to the end, that the number may be
rightly appropriated to any multitude
propos'd, according as the thing re-
quires.　But this does not at all
come within the reach of the material faculty, with which Brutes are
only endued.

97. Since therefore number is not
properly form'd but by the Intellect,
which *Aristotle* himself confesseth, 4.
Phyf. t. 131. it must necessarily follow, that the names of Number are
only repeated by the Memory in
Brutes

Brutes that name it, but the Essence of Number, or difference, of the fourth, and fifth, or twentieth, is not in them.

98. As to the Writing of Inanimate Creatures, since that *Elephants* use the *Probofcis*, as a Hand, and almost as readily as we do (for they will take the smallest peice of Money off from the ground, and ordinarily manage a Sword like a Fencer, handle a Gun, level it and discharge, as we our selves, that have been eye-witnesses, can testify) it need not seem an impossibility for them to Write some Letters, whose figures they have been taught, either singly, or joyntly, and so reduced them into words, and perhaps by Writing to expreſs their conception of any particular thing according to custom, as other Brutes use to notify their conceptions by gestures, or other wayes suitable to their nature.

99. But it is sufficiently apparent by what hath been said, how infinitely the

the Speech of Inanimate Creatures, and the adumbration thereof by Writing, doth differ from Human Speech; whereas Man doth not appropriate this, or that word, to this, or that particular thing by custom only; but can use his Tongue volubly, and can exercise it in the expressing of any thing whatsoever, upon all emergent occasions, in a far different manner from that of Brutes : And as Mans Reason it self, or the internal Speech, doth not only aim at particular and material, but universal, abstracted, and immaterial things, which Brutes by their Reason cannot do, so the external Speech, which is the *nuncius* of the internal, is assisted thereby, which indeed the Speech of Brutes cannot aspire unto.

100. So that there is, as vast a distance between the Reason of Inanimate Creatures and Humane Reason, and their Speech, or the signification of things which is designed by Speech, and the Speech of Man, as there

there is between the Material and Immaterial Faculty. And therefore we may truly conclude, that no Creature is endued with the faculty of real Speech, or true Reason, but Man only; but the Speech of Brutes may be said faintly to resemble the true Speech of Man, as also their Reason, Human Reason, by some kind of Analogy.

FINIS.

Books

Books Printed for William Crook, at the green Dragon without Temple-Bar.

Praxis Curiæ Admiralitatis Angliæ, *Authore Fransc. Cherk*. Printed 1667. price bound 1 s.

The Compleat Measurer, or an exact new way of Mensuration, by which may be measured both Superficies and Solids in whole Numbers and Fractions, in a more plain and easy way, than ever yet extant, whereby you may find out the Contents of all superficies and solids in whole numbers and fractions by the help of Multiplication, without Division, by *Tho. Hammond*. in 8° price bound 1 s.

A Voyage into the *Levant*, being a brief Journey lately performed from *England* by the way of *Venice* into *Dalmatia*, *Sclavonia*, *Bosna*, *Hungary*, *Macedonia*, *Thessaly*, *Thrace*, *Rhodes* and *Ægypt*, unto *Gran Cairo*, with par-

particular obfervations concerning the modern Condition of the *Turks*, and other People under that Empire, by Sr. *Henry Blunt* Knight; in 12° Printed 1669. price bound 1 s.

A Tract concerning Schifm and Schifmaticks, wherein is briefly difcovered the original Caufes of all Schifm, written by the late Learned and Judicious Divine *Iohn Hales* of *Eaton*; in 4to. 6 d.

Hugonis Grotii Baptizatorium; Puerorum Inftitutio alternis interrogationibus & refponfionibus : Cai adjicitur Græca ejufdem Metaphrafis à Chrifto : Wafe Regalis Colleg. Cant. una cum obfervatiunculis in Græcam Metaphrafin ad Calcem appenfis : Quibus acceffit praxis in Græcam Metaphrafin per B. Beale *cum Græcis Teftimoniis ex facra pagina & Indice locupletiffimo*, in 8o Printed 1668. price bound 2s.

The Court of Curiofity, wherein by the *Algebra* and Lott the moft intricate queftions are refolved, and Nocturnal Dreams and Vifions explained,

plained, according to the doctrine of the Antients; to which is also added a Treatise of *Physiognomy*: published in *French* by *Mark de Vulson* Kt. of the Order of *S. Michael*, and Gentleman in ordinary to the *French* King, (since translated into *Spanish*, *Italian*, and *Dutch*, and now) into *English*, by *I. G.* Gent. of the Inner *Temple*, in 8° Printed 1670. price bound 2 s.

A description of *Candia* in its antient and modern state, with an account of the siege thereof begun by the *Ottoman* Emperour in the year 1666. continued 1667, 1668. and surrendred the latter end of 1669. in 8° printed 1670. price bound 1 s.

The Compleat Vinyeard, or an excellent way for planting of Vines according to the *German* and *French* manner and long practised in *England*, wherein is set forth the wayes and all the circumstances necessary for planting of a Vineyard, with the election of the soil, the scituation thereof, the best way for planting the young plants,
the

the beſt time and manner of pruning the turning & tranſlation of the ground &c. with other obſervations, alſo the faſhion of Wine-preſſes, the manner of bruiſing and preſſing Grapes, and how to advance our *Engliſh* Vines, enlarged above half by the Author *W. Hughs* ; 8o, printed 1670. price 1s.6d.

Epigrams of all ſorts made at divers times, and ſeveral occaſions by *R. F.* 8o printed 1670. price bound 1 s.

Sylva ſylvarum, or a natural Hiſtory in ten Centuries, whereunto is newly added the Hiſtory Natural and Experimental of Life and Death, or the prolongation of Life, publiſhed after the Authors death by *W. Rawley* D.D. one of His Majeſt. Chapl. whereunto is added Articles of Inquiry touching Minerals, and the new *Melantis, as alſo the Life of the Author*, never added to this Book before, written by the Right honourable *Francis* Lord *Verulam*, Viſcount *St. Alban*, the ninth and laſt Edition, with an Alphabetical Table of the principal things contained in the ten

ten Centuries. fol. printed 1670. pr. 8s.

The Triumph of Gods revenge a-
gainft the crying and execrable fin of
Murther, &c. In 30 feveral hiftories, de-
livered by *J. Reynolds*, 5 Edition with
pictures, fol. printed 1670. price 10s.

The Jefuites Morals collected by a
Doctor of the Colledge of *Sorbonn* in
Paris, who hath faithfully extracted
them out of the Jefuites own Books
which are printed by the permiffion &
approbation of the fuperior of their
Society tranflated out of *French* in folio
printed 1670. price bound 10s.

A Sermon Preached at the funeral of
a fober Religious Man found drowned
in a Pit not long ago, enlarged by the
Author upon his review, in 8° printed
1670. price bound 1s.

The Deaf and Dumb mans Difcourfe, or a
Treatife concerning thofe that are born deaf
and dumb, containing a difcovery of their
Knowledge or Underftanding, as alfo the Method they ufe, to manifeft the fentiments of
of their minds together with an additional
tract of the Reafon and Speech of inanimate
Creatures, by *G. Sibfcota*; 8° printed 1670.
price bound 1s.